City of Snow

The Great Blizzard of 1888

Linda Oatman High

Illustrations by Laura Francesca Filippucci

WALKER & COMPANY
NEW YORK

It was Sunday morning,
March 11, 1888, and rain was falling,
spraying a steady tempest from heaven.

It drenched our heads
and my best dress
as Mama and Papa and I left church,
        umbrella-less.

Purple and yellow crocuses shone
in the stone gray afternoon.
Springtime would soon arrive in
the city of New York.

The windows of stores were glorious,
with mannequins wearing the springtime
        fashions
as we rushed past,
splashing and dashing through the wet
        weather,
hurrying home to a Sunday dinner
at the dismal end of winter.

It rained buckets all Sunday,
and our roof began to leak.
Our kitchen floor sopping,
I prayed while I mopped,
for the rain to stop.
Tomorrow morning was P. T. Barnum's circus expedition.
I'd been saving my money for the fifty-cent admission.

Bargaining with Mama and God,
I promised to be good
and to cheerfully complete every chore,
if only I could see Barnum's most famous tour:
"The Finest Assembly of Trained Animals Since Noah,"
the newspaper did assure.

Gazing at the rain making a lake of New York
in the fast-growing dark,
I thought perhaps Papa should build us an ark
so we'd be sure to embark
on our circus-day lark.

By nightfall the rain had turned to snow,
and gutters churned with slush.
Sleet balls plinked across our roofs,
above the house's nighttime hush,
ice clip-clopping like a hundred horses' hooves.

Howling winds rattled the windows
like careless thieves,
and the eaves wheezed,
heaving as if the house were breathing.

I slept as fitful as the wind
and woke shivering in the night.
The temperature had dipped,
and whips of coldness crept
through cracks in the plaster wall.

Quivering in my quilt,
I saw a sliver of white through my window,
pale as a pitcher of milk.

I leaped from my bed at daybreak,
and ran straight to look out my window.
What was below made my eyes ache:
the blinding white of a city of snow.

There were no roads,
no wagons hauling loads,
no ponies,
no paper,
no people,
no milk,
no meat,
no streets,
no trains on tracks,
no teams, no hacks,
no sidewalks, no paths,
no *thing* but snow.

Papa couldn't get to his job,
and our old horse, Bob,
was too hobbled and wobbly legged
to pull our carriage through the drifts to the show.

Gentle Bob stood
patiently waiting
for me to come skating
with apples and carrots
to his stable.
His dappled back rippled
as he whinnied and trembled.

I whispered in Bob's ear,
telling him not to fear.
Even though the snow was fiercely wild,
I was sure that the weather would soon turn mild.

It was only a few blocks
to Madison Square,
so I begged Papa for us to walk there.

Bundled in boots and wool,
scarves and gloves and hats,
Mama and Papa and I
ventured outside like nervous cats
but plodding like mules.

Bitten by a bitter wind
as we trudged in slow single file,
we pushed and leaned,
seeing crushed storefronts
and sparrows frozen in snow,
blown and tangled telegraph wires.

We walked and walked,
and as we trudged along,
I crossed my fingers
and hoped
that P. T. Barnum's show
would go on.

We finally arrived
at Madison Square,
happily relieved
that the circus was there.

Lions and tigers and bears,
a daring girl on a high-flying trapeze,
a clown with a red-nosed sneeze,
dancing dogs and prancing ponies,
eighty-six fabulous acts in all.

"The storm may be a great show,"
said Mister Barnum, in all his mirth,
"but I still have the greatest show on
    Earth!"

Applause scattered
within the almost-empty big top,
and all that mattered
was that the fun would never stop.

When the circus ended,
we left the red tent
and stepped, bent,
into the quick icy wind
as hats and trash whipped
from the wind's wicked lash.

Our faces glazed crystal,
we battled the blizzard,
which was like a wild animal
rattling a cage,
attacking and fighting
all in a rage.

The trolleys and trains
could not move,
and passengers were rescued,
their faces white-blue.

My lungs squeezed,
and I could hardly breathe,
as we hiked slowly
toward home.

We huddled by the stove
and peeled off clothes that had froze.
We decided to make the blizzard
an occasion of celebration
by having our own
snow-party jubilation.

Eating snow ice-cream with syrup,
savoring the sweet, frosty flavor,
Mama and Papa and I made party favors
and played games with neighbors.

Some whittled, some fiddled,
some told riddles
or sang hearty old songs
to pass the time along.

All day Monday,
all Monday night,
all day Tuesday,
all Tuesday night,
the blizzard continued
its sharp, icy bite,
coating the city
with a blanket of white.

The street outside was covered
in wires from a fallen pole,
and we were running low
on milk and meat and coal.

Now the blizzard
wasn't as much fun
as it had been
when first begun.

B y Wednesday
pedestrians tested their muscles,
attempting to bustle through
high piles of drifted snow.
But swiftly whirling winter winds
twirled them like little dolls.

Bulky in layers of clothing,
the walkers wore blizzard fashions
dug from trunks hunkered in attics:
dusty and musty hats and caps,
skins of cats, bears, and muskrats
all joined the scarves and mittens of
    many colors
whisked away by winter winds,
looking pretty as they littered the city.

The blizzard ended Wednesday night,
leaving behind a city of white.

It was early Thursday,
and, not caring what others said,
I wrapped a bed blanket around my head
and kept my face warm
with a rag of faded red.

We stepped through the door,
into a world that was magic:
snow making strange shapes, like waves,
and shovelers digging paths for sleighs.

Pranksters buried boots and trousers
upside down in high snowbanks,
and once I stumbled over what was only
a lonely wooden Indian that tumbled
from the porch of a cigar store.

A tunnel was dug to Lugman's Drugs,
in a drift on Sixth Avenue,
and I crawled through,
buying a blue pitcher of fizzy,
famous Blakely's Blizzard Soda.

On Friday
merchants and churches
made posters and signs,
joking about free snow
for those passing by.

There were still no deliveries of food or coal,
and we were wishing for steak and milk and eggs.
Mama made bread and kept us well fed,
and just before bed
a red-capped head appeared outside the window.

It was the milkman, Fred,
driving a horse-drawn sled,
gliding high on top of a totally frozen drift.

Fred knocked on the glass,
and we all laughed,
glad to finally have milk.

On Saturday
black rollers of steel
packed down the snow,
strong horses snorting and snuffling,
their hooves shuffling,
moving slow.

Numb from the cold,
shoveling rolled
and heavy snow,
every household
helped to load
cartfuls of snow,
to be taken below
the city roads
and dumped into the river.

Shivering,
I wished that this mess
would soon be over.

It was Sunday again,
after the blizzard that wouldn't end.
A thaw had melted most of the snow,
and gutters were churning with slush.

Icicles dripped as walkers slipped
on slick streets, greeting each other
with tired smiles.

Sunshine peeked
from the gloomy sky
for the first time in a week,
and I knew that crocuses would
once more bloom,
and we'd go back to school soon.

Splashing home from church,
my best shoes were wet,
and I knew I'd never forget
the city of snow,
the terrible Great Blizzard of 1888.

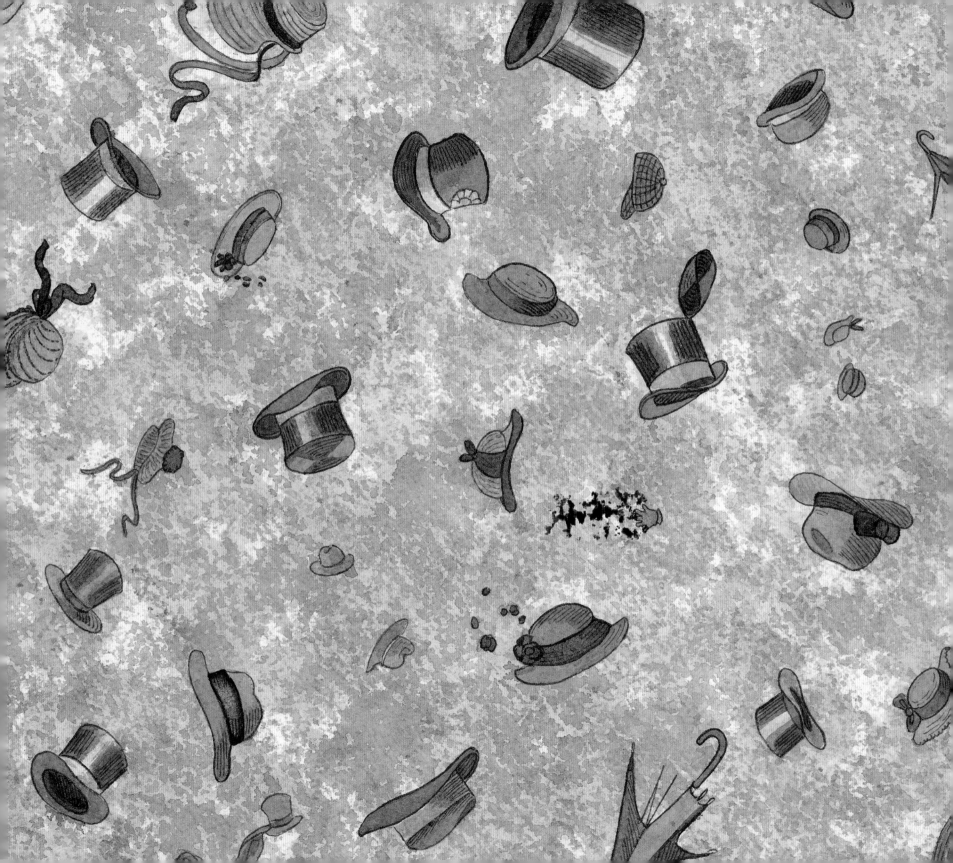